A Monster for Tea

by Walter Williams

A Monster for Tea by Walter Williams
published by Fernwood and Hedges Books (2013)
First Edition
Library of Congress Control Number: 2013946533
ISBN: 978-0-9890698-3-0

For Dasha

In the dark of night, a monster crept through a flower garden. And, being a monster, he was neither careful nor quiet and woke the little girl whose garden he had just trampled.

Stop right where you are! said the little girl. How dare you creep across my garden? Do not take another step with your giant monster feet!

The monster's eyes widened with surprise for he had never been spoken to this way, especially by a little girl. But, he did stop, and without turning to face the little girl, stepped out and over the flower bed and headed towards the forest.

Wait! Come back! said the little girl.

People run from me. They most certainly do not call me back, said the monster.

Why are you not afraid?
asked the monster.

Because I'm not afraid of monsters.

Would you like some tea?
asked the little girl.

The monster had never had tea. In fact, he did not know what it was. He only knew about eating people and animals and tearing apart buildings and breathing fire.

The little girl brought a
chair so the monster could
sit.

But the chair was much too small to accommodate his size.

So, he plopped down on the ground.

The little girl brought tea and cookies.

But the monster was unable to
hold the cup.

So, the little girl helped
the monster drink.

Soon, the tea pot was empty and the cookies were gone. The monster laid back and rubbed his belly and looked up at the stars.

The little girl brought a blanket and said goodnight with a kiss upon the monster's spikey head.
The monster thought, as he looked up at the girl with his large bulbous eyes, no one has ever been so kind.

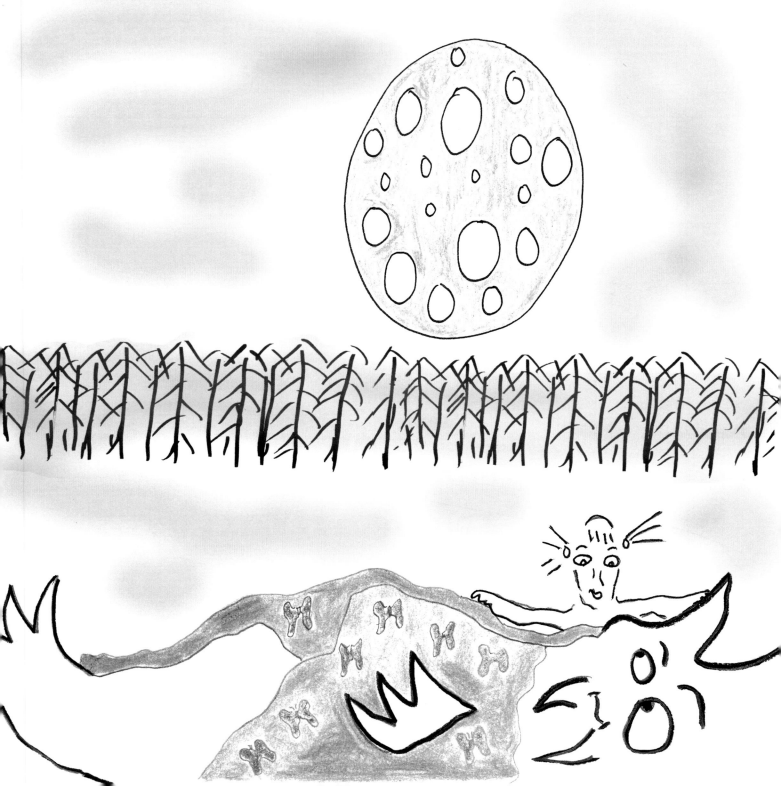

And, as the little girl looked down from the upstairs window on the monster sleeping peacefully below, she wondered if he'd forgotten about eating people and animals and tearing apart buildings and breathing fire.

CPSIA information can be obtained
at www.ICGtesting.com
Printed in the USA
LVXC01n1432290414
383723LV00007B/11